A NOTE TO PARENTS

When your children are ready to "step into reading," giving them the right books is as crucial to their development as giving them the right food to eat. **Step into Reading®** books feature exciting stories and information reinforced with lively, colorful illustrations that make learning to read fun, satisfying, and rewarding. We have even taken *extra* steps to keep your child engaged by offering Step into Reading Sticker books, Step into Reading Math books, and Step into Reading Phonics books, in addition to fabulous fiction and nonfiction.

Learning to read, Step by Step:

- **Super Early** books (Preschool–Kindergarten) support pre-reading skills. Parent and child can engage in "see and say" reading using the strong picture cues and the few simple words on each page.
- **Early** books (Preschool–Kindergarten) let emergent readers tackle one or two short sentences of large type per page.
- **Step 1** books (Preschool–Grade 1) have the same easy-to-read type as Early, but with more words per page.
- **Step 2** books (Grades 1–3) offer longer and slightly more difficult text while introducing contractions and clauses. Children are often drawn to our exciting natural science nonfiction titles at this level.
- **Step 3** books (Grades 2–3) present paragraphs, chapters, and fully developed plot lines in fiction and nonfiction.
- **Step 4** books (Grades 2–4) feature thrilling nonfiction illustrated with exciting photographs for independent as well as reluctant readers.

Remember: The grade levels assigned to the six steps are intended only as guides. Some children move through all six steps rapidly; others climb the steps over a period of a few years. Either way, these books will help children "step into reading" for life!

To Paul, who has the biggest heart
—J. W.

www.randomhouse.com/kids/disney

Library of Congress Cataloging-in-Publication Data
Weinberg, Jennifer Liberts, 1970–
Piglet feels small/ by Jennifer Liberts Weinberg ;
    p.   cm. — (Early step into reading)
SUMMARY: Piglet feels sad because he's too small to climb trees or fly kites until his friends remind
him of the many things he can do.
ISBN 0-7364-1226-3
[1. Size —Fiction. 2. Pigs—Fiction. 3. Toys—Fiction. 4. Stories in rhyme.] I. Milne, A. A.
(Alan Alexander), 1882–1956. Winnie the Pooh. II. Title. III. Series.
PZ8.3.L597 Pi 2001
[E]—dc21
2001019778

Printed in the United States of America   January 2002   10 9 8 7 6 5 4 3 2 1

Step into Reading®

Disney
Winnie the Pooh

Piglet Feels Small

An Early Book

By Jennifer Liberts Weinberg

Illustrated by Josie Yee

Random House New York

Pooh can climb a tree!

Piglet is too small
to climb a tree.

Tigger can bounce high.

Piglet is too small
to bounce high.

Christopher Robin
can fly a kite.

Oh, dear!
Piglet is too small
to fly a kite.

"I am too small
to do anything at all!"
says Piglet.

Pooh tells his sad friend,
"But look at all
that you <u>can</u> do."

"You can pick berries,"
says Pooh.

"You can plant seeds,"
says Pooh.

Piglet is a big help
to Rabbit.

"Yes!" says Piglet.
"And I can share
with you and Eeyore."

"I can play

Pooh Sticks."

"And I can count!"
Piglet shouts.

"I can hum a sunny tune
with you . . .

. . . and play

follow-the-leader, too!"

When someone is sad,

being small is not bad.

Piglet can give big hugs,

and make a friend smile!

Piglet always goes
the extra mile.

Piglet is small,

that is true . . .

. . . but he can do
lots of things,
just like you!